My First Sea Turtle Book

JENNY KELLETT

BELLANOVA

MELBOURNE · SOFIA · BERLIN

My name is...

Hey
there!
I'm
Shelly
the sea
turtle.

Sea turtles live in the ocean.

Can you find me in the ocean?

Sea turtles live in oceans
all around the world,
but they prefer warm,
tropical water.

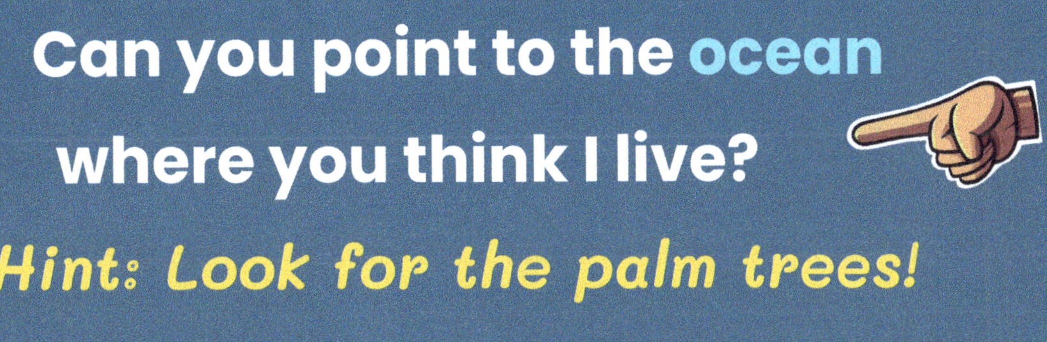

Can you point to the ocean where you think I live?
Hint: Look for the palm trees!

Sea turtles have special flippers to help them swim.

Can you count how many flippers I have?
1
2
3
4

Sea turtles have strong, hard shells to protect them.

My ocean friends also have shells!

Can you <u>match</u> them to their shadows?

Mmm,
yummy!
Sea turtles love to eat
jellyfish and seaweed.

Do you know which of these animals is a jellyfish?
Hint: It's very jiggly!

Sea turtles are very quiet. Shhhh....

...but the ocean is full of sounds. Can you help make some ocean sounds?

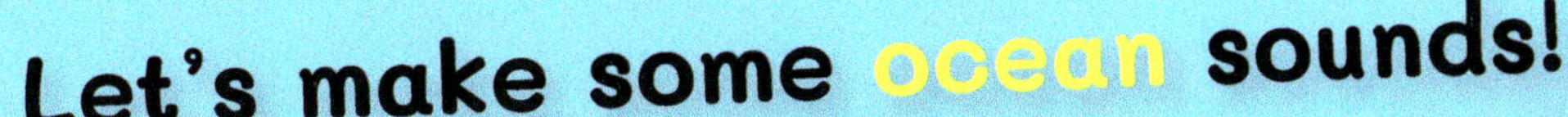

Let's make some ocean sounds!

Can you say: Splish Splash!

Woosh! Bubble Bubble!?

Sea turtles prefer to live alone.

My favorite activities....

Swimming

Eating

Point to the pictures of
what you like to do too!

Exploring

Hiding

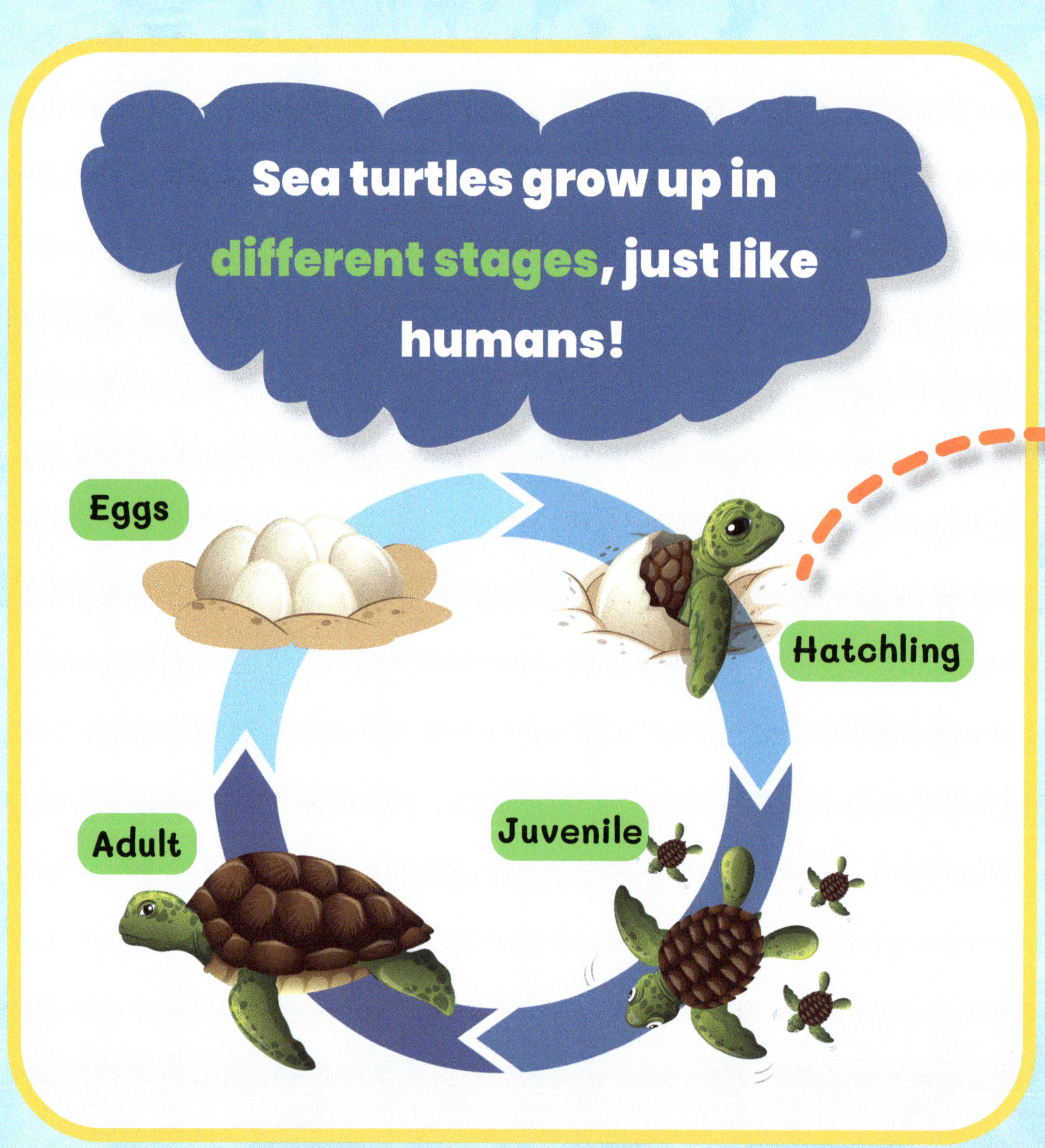

Sea turtles grow up in different stages, just like humans!
Eggs
Hatchling
Adult
Juvenile

Which stage is this turtle in?

Turtle babies are called hatchlings.
They are tiny and very cute!

Chicken

Penguin

Duck

Sea turtles lay their eggs on the beach!

After 9 weeks, the hatchlings are born and they make their way to the ocean.

Let's count together!
Can you tell me how many eggs I have in my nest?

Sea turtles need our help! They can get hurt by plastic in the ocean and can get trapped in fishing nets.

You can help sea turtles by recycling plastic and keeping the oceans and beaches clean.

Shelly needs your help!

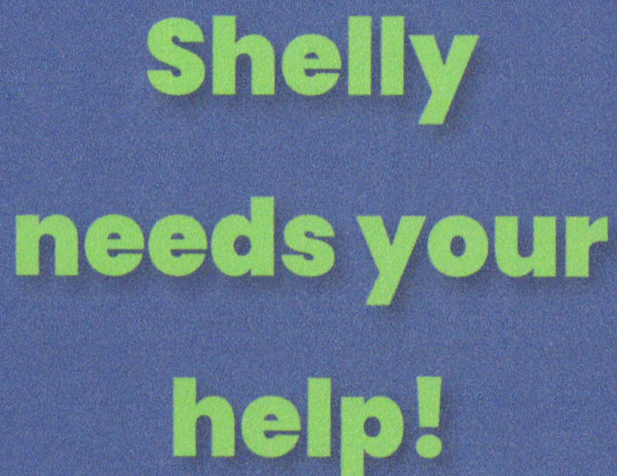

The ocean is full of things that can hurt sea turtles. Can you find the **bad things?**

Circle the items that can hurt sea turtles.

What is your favorite thing about sea turtles?

Can you name two foods that sea turtles eat?

How can we help keep sea turtles safe?

Congratulations!

Name: ....

For learning all about

SEA TURTLES

And becoming a Sea Turtle Expert

Jenny Kellett
Author

ALSO BY JENNY KELLETT

Find us on **YouTube** for weekly animal videos just for kids!

... and more!

Available at
www.bellanovabooks.com
and all major online bookstores.

* 9 7 8 2 4 8 7 1 9 1 1 8 1 *